For Sam, and the adventures, discoveries, and feasts that lie ahead

Thank you to Catherine for helping Magnus come to life

First U.S. edition 2020
First published by Otter-Barry Books (U.K.) 2019

Library of Congress Catalog Card Number pending
ISBN 978-1-5362-1352-2

19 20 21 22 23 24 TLF 10 9 8 7 6 5 4 3 2 1

Printed in Dongguan, Guangdong, China

This book was typeset in Big Caslon.
The illustrations were done in watercolor and lithography with digital rendering.

Candlewick Press
99 Dover Street
Somerville, Massachusetts 02144

visit us at www.candlewick.com

What's that Noise?

Naomi Howarth

CANDLEWICK PRESS

Early one morning, while the sun was rising over the icy plains of the Arctic, a long, low rumbling sound woke Magnus from a very deep sleep.

"What's that noise?" he wondered.

rumble

rumble

rumble

Could it be the wind?

Could it be the sea?

Could it be an iceberg cracking?

Magnus just couldn't figure it out.

He needed to find a friend with a
good pair of ears. . . .

"Hello, Hare!" said Magnus.
"Can you help me? What's that noise?"

Hare listened. . . . .

rumble

rumble

"I don't know," said Hare.
"But let's go and ask our friends."

rumble

rumble

rumble

So Magnus and Hare set off over the ice,
and all the while, the rumbling sound followed them.

By the frosty forest, they met Owl.

"Hello, Owl," Magnus said. "Can you help us?
What's that noise? Is it the creaking of the trees?"

rumble

rumble

rumble

Owl listened.

"Oh, no," she said.
"It's not the creaking
of the trees."

On top of the snowy rocks, they met Fox.

"Hello, Fox," said Magnus. "Can you help us?
What's that noise? Is it the whistling of the wind?"

rumble

rumble

rumble

Fox listened.
"Oh, no," he said. "It's not the whistling of the wind."

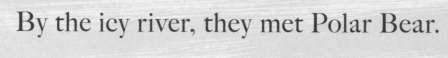

By the icy river, they met Polar Bear.

"Hello, Bear. Can you help us? What's that noise?
Is it the cracking of the ice?"

rumble

rumble

Bear listened.
"Oh, no," she said. "It's not the cracking of the ice."

rumble

At last, by the edge of the sea, they met Walrus.

"Please, Walrus, can you help us? What's that noise?
Is it the roaring of the sea?"

rumble

rumble

rumble

"Oh, no," said Walrus. "It's not the roaring of the sea . . .
but I think I know what it could be.

Dive into the water and catch the plumpest,
pinkest shrimp you can find."

With a SPLASH, Magnus dived down, down to the depths of the sea.

And there he found lots of plump pink shrimp.

He brought them back to Walrus,
and they had a delicious feast.

Suddenly, they realized that it was very quiet.

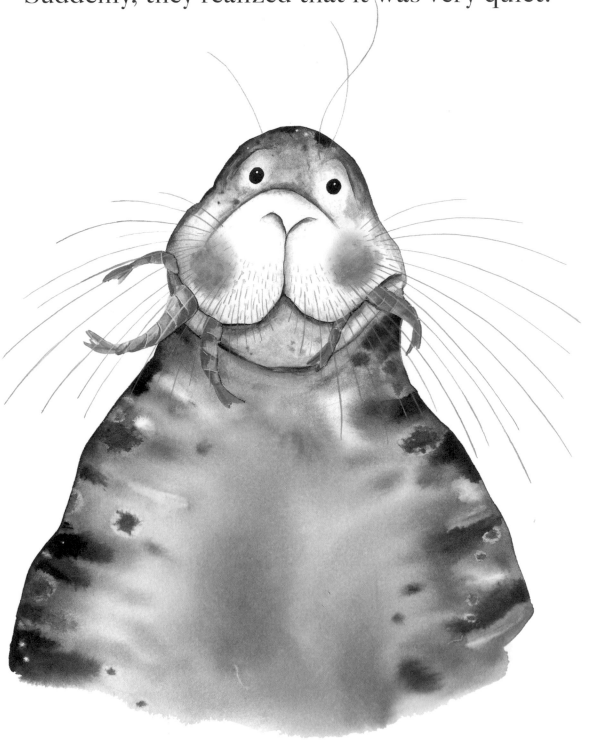

The noise had STOPPED!

"It wasn't the creaking of the trees
or the whistling of the wind," said Magnus.

"And it wasn't the cracking of the ice
or the roaring of the sea.

The great rumbling sound
has been coming from —

ME!"

And everyone laughed to think of ALL that noise coming from Magnus's rumbling, grumbling HUNGRY TUMMY!

So after their long day and with their tummies full, the friends settled down to a deep sleep.

It was very peaceful.

But then . . .

Walrus peeled open one wrinkly eye.
"WHAT'S THAT NOISE?"

rumble

It was the long, loud rumbling
sound of sleepy seal snores.

rumble

rumble

Good night, Magnus!

The Arctic

The Arctic is a vast frozen area centered around the North Pole. It's mostly ice-covered ocean but does include some dry land—parts of North America, Greenland, Europe, and Asia. With the warming of Earth's climate, the ice cover is becoming smaller each year, making life increasingly difficult for the animals and birds that live on the sea ice and shorelines.

Ringed Seal

Ringed seals are named for the light-colored circular markings on their coat, which become more prominent as the seals age. Female seals dig ice caves to raise their pups in, protecting them from storms and polar bears. But with Arctic warming, making ice caves has become difficult, and pups are sometimes born on bare ice with no protection.

Arctic Fox

Arctic foxes have a thick, fluffy coat that keeps them cozy in temperatures as low as −58°F/−50°C. Their fur coat turns from gray in the summer to white in winter, providing them with effective camouflage throughout the year.

Arctic Hare

Arctic hares have long black eyelashes that protect their eyes from the sun—like very special sunglasses!

Baby Arctic Hare

Baby Arctic hares are called leverets. They can have up to eight brothers and sisters, making life very busy for Mommy Hare!